CONTENTS

HEiDi HECKELBECK

Has a New Best Friend

By Wanda Coven

Illustrated by Priscilla Burris

LITTLE SIMON

New York London Toronto Sydney New Delhi

This book is a work of fiction. Any references to historical events, real people, or real places are used fictitiously. Other names, characters, places, and events are products of the author's imagination, and any resemblance to actual events or places or persons, living or dead, is entirely coincidental.

LITTLE SIMON
An imprint of Simon & Schuster Children's Publishing Division
1230 Avenue of the Americas, New York, New York 10020
First Little Simon hardcover edition January 2018
Copyright © 2018 by Simon & Schuster, Inc.
Also available in a Little Simon paperback edition.

Designed by Ciara Gay
Manufactured in the United States of America 1217 FFG
10 9 8 7 6 5 4 3 2 1
Library of Congress Cataloging-in-Publication Data
Names: Coven, Wanda, author.
Title: Heidi Heckelbeck has a new best friend / by Wanda Coven ; illustrated by Priscilla Burris.
Description: First Little Simon paperback edition. | New York : Little Simon, 2018. | Series: Heidi Heckelbeck ; 22 | Summary: "Heidi's new neighbor wants to become Heidi's best friend"— Provided by publisher.
Identifiers: LCCN 2017016650 | ISBN 9781534411074 (paperback) | ISBN 9781534411081 (hc) | ISBN 9781534411098 (eBook)
Subjects: | CYAC: Best friends—Fiction. | Friendship—Fiction. | Magic—Fiction. | Witches—Fiction. | BISAC: JUVENILE FICTION / Fantasy & Magic. | JUVENILE FICTION / Imagination & Play. | JUVENILE FICTION / Readers / Chapter Books.
Classification: LCC PZ7.C83393 Hdt 2018 | DDC [Fic]—dc23
LC record available at https://lccn.loc.gov/2017016650

Chapter 1

SPY GUY

"Ha-a-a hu-u-um," Heidi yawned.

She rubbed her eyes and padded across the kitchen in her bunny slippers and pink polka-dot pajamas. It was a quiet and peaceful morning. Heidi loved to have breakfast in her pj's every Sunday.

But she didn't love it when Henry
acted like an unexpected alarm clock.

"GUESS WHAT!" Henry yelled as he
walked through the back door.

Heidi was so surprised, she spilled
her milk.

Henry didn't even make fun of her, so the whole family knew he must have big news. "We have NEW NEIGHBORS!"

Heidi wiped up the mess. "We do?"
Henry put his hands on his hips proudly. "Yep. There's a moving truck and everything. RIGHT. NEXT. DOOR."

Heidi's bunny slippers hopped
across the floor as she ran to the
window to see.

"You're right!" she cried.

"TOLD YOU!" Henry said. "I've been
spying on them ever since I got up."

Mom set her teacup on her saucer. "HENRY!" she scolded. "It's not polite to *spy*."

Henry shrugged. "But, Mom, how else am I going to find out important stuff, like that they have a GIANT trampoline?"

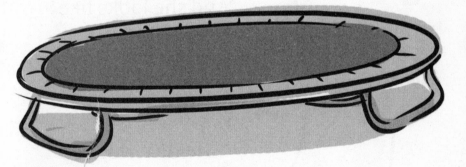

Mom frowned. "Nobody likes a snoop, young man."

Heidi whirled around. "I DO!" she announced. "Especially if there are trampolines involved. Hey, snoop! Do they have any KIDS?"

Henry nodded. "A *GIRL*," he said as he made a gross face. "And she looks like she's your age. I heard her mom call her Bryce."

Heidi clapped her hands. "Yay!" she cried. "I wonder if we'll be friends!"

Heidi always dreamed of having a
friend next door. Then she had an
idea. "Mom, can we bake chocolate
chip cookies for our new neighbors?"
she asked excitedly.

"I think that sounds sweet, Heidi," her mom said with a smile. "But listen up, Henry. It's time to stop your spy-guy game. You're going to be on cookie patrol with your sister."

Henry and Heidi stood up straight and gave Mom a salute. Operation: Welcome to the Neighborhood was a go.

Chapter 2

BRYCE IS NiCE!

Ding-dong!

Ding-dong!

Ding-dong!

Henry rang the new neighbors' doorbell three times in a row.

"Please stop ding-donging!" Heidi said. "It's not good manners!"

Henry giggled. "I can't help it. I love pressing doorbells."

A girl with long black hair and bangs opened the door.

"Welcome to the neighborhood!" Heidi said, looking the girl up and down. She had on a navy-and-white-striped outfit and matching flats with an adorable ankle strap.

"What cute shoes!" Heidi exclaimed.

The girl glanced at her feet and back at Heidi. "Thanks," she said, smiling.

Then the girl's mother and father came to the door.

"We're the Beltrans," said the mom.

"Nice to meet you. We're the Heckelbecks from next door," Heidi's mom said.

Heidi remembered the cookies and held them out. "And I'm Heidi."

Mrs. Beltran accepted the cookies. "How thoughtful," she said. "This is our daughter, Bryce."

Heidi waved, but Bryce took a step
behind her mother.

Then the parents began to talk
with one another. Heidi asked Bryce
what grade she was in.

"Second," Bryce said. "What about you?"

"Same!" Heidi said.

Their parents and Henry the spy went inside while the girls sat down on the stoop.

"Who's your teacher?" Heidi asked.

"Mrs. Rayburn."

Heidi stuck out her front lip. "Oh merg. I have Mrs. Welli—the other second-grade teacher. But they're both really nice. And we'll still have lunch and recess together."

Bryce nodded and stayed quiet.

"Would you like a tour of the neighborhood?" asked Heidi.

"Sure," said Bryce.

After getting their parents' permission, Heidi showed Bryce around. They rode their scooters to the bus stop and to the park. The girls climbed the monkey bars and chatted some more.

"So, tell me what are some of your favorite things?" Heidi asked.

Bryce sat on a bar. "Hmm, well, pink is my favorite color."

Heidi's was yellow.

"And my favorite food is cheesy enchiladas."

Heidi's was pizza.

"Hmm, let's see. Do you have favorite book?" Heidi asked.

"Yes! *Charlotte's Web*," Bryce said. "Which is weird because I hate spiders."

That made Heidi laugh. "Hey, you know what? That is my favorite book too!"

For the rest of the day Bryce shared every favorite thing she could think of, and Heidi didn't mind a bit. She was so happy to have a new friend—right next door.

"Thanks for the tour!" Bryce said, parking her scooter outside her back porch. "I had SO much fun!"

"Me too!" Heidi said. "See you in the morning!"

Heidi totally understood. She was about to say that the only flashy dresser at Brewster Elementary was Melanie Maplethorpe, but Bryce kept right on talking.

MOTORMOUTH

Heidi zoomed to the bus stop the next day. She wanted to make sure she was there first. Bryce skipped down the sidewalk in a pink skirt, white tee, and gray cardigan. She even had on matching gray booties.

"Hi!" called Heidi as the bus pulled

up and the doors folded open.

"Hey," said Bryce as they lined up to board. She grabbed Heidi by the arm and chattered away.

"It took me FOREVER to pick an outfit for my FIRST day of school," Bryce said. She stood back. "Do you like it?"

Heidi was about to say *I LOVE it,* but Bryce didn't give her a chance.

"I didn't want to look too flashy," Bryce went on, "but I didn't want to look too plain, either. It's so hard to decide when you're new, you know?"

"At my OLD school, there was this super-stylish group of girls," she said. "They always wore the latest fashions. There was this one girl who even wore sunglasses to school, and—get this—she wore them INSIDE the building. Can you believe that?"

Heidi slid onto a seat and scooched over to make room for Bryce. She was about to ask Bryce about her old school, but just as she opened her mouth, Bryce rattled on.

"And that very same girl was on the cheerleading team with me," she said. "Now that I think about it, she was really actually nice—just kind of spoiled, if you know what I mean. Anyway, are you a cheerleader, Heidi?"

Bryce tucked a strand of hair behind her ear and waited briefly for an answer.

"Um, no," Heidi managed to say.

"Well, I think cheerleaders have one of the MOST important jobs in the whole school," she explained.

"That's because they have to be LEADERS. They also have to have TONS of spirit—PLUS they have to be amazing dancers and tumblers. *Did you know all that?*"

Heidi nodded as the bus pulled in to the next stop. She waved to her friends Lucy Lancaster and Bruce Bickerson as they boarded the bus.

Bryce didn't notice and went right on talking as if Lucy and Bruce weren't even there.

"So, what else do you like to do for fun, Heidi?" Bryce asked. But again, she didn't leave time for Heidi to answer.

"Well, I like to make crafts, play the guitar, ride my scooter, play board games, read, draw with sidewalk chalk, and bake," Bryce said. "Did you know I just learned how to make blueberry muffins all by myself? They came out so yummy. Do you like to bake?"

Heidi opened her mouth and . . .

"OH YEAH!" blurted Bryce. "You DO like to bake. I know because you made scrummy chocolate chip cookies for us. Did you know 'scrummy' is a cross between 'scrumptious' and 'yummy'? GET IT?"

Heidi nodded as the bus finally pulled into the drop-off lane.

"By the way, would you take me to Principal Pennypacker's office?" Bryce asked. "I'm supposed to go there first thing."

Heidi sighed. "Sure," she said. "No problem."

Heidi dropped Bryce off at the principal's office and walked to her classroom, but she didn't go inside. Instead, she leaned against the wall to rest. Lucy and Bruce saw her standing outside the classroom door and hurried over.

"There you are!" Lucy said.

Bruce shrugged off his backpack. "Who was that girl you were with?"

Heidi breathed in deeply. "That was my new next-door neighbor. Her

name is Bryce, and she's really nice
and very talkative." Heidi patted her
ears to make sure they hadn't fallen
off.

Lucy and Bruce laughed.

"Well, she's probably just excited about going to a new school," Lucy said.

"Probably," Heidi said as they entered the classroom. Then Heidi thought back to her first day at Brewster. Being new hadn't made her talkative. It had made her kind of quiet. And right now all she wanted was quiet.

OUCH!

Boppity!

Boppity!

Bop!

Melanie Maplethorpe's blond hair bopped up and down as she pranced through the hallway to lunch.

"Wait UP, you guys!" Melanie called.

Then she boppity-bopped right up to Heidi, Lucy, and Bruce.

"SO!" she said. "Who's this NEW girl I keep hearing about?" Melanie looked right at Heidi. She seemed to know Heidi had the scoop.

"Her name is Bryce Beltran," Heidi said, "and she moved in next door to me."

Melanie gasped. "Oh, that POOR girl! Does she know she moved in next door to a WEIRDO?"

Heidi felt her face flush.

Melanie laughed and skipped down the hall toward Stanley Stonewrecker.

"Oh MERG!" Heidi grumbled. "That girl makes me SO mad."

Lucy patted Heidi on the shoulder. "Don't let her get to you. That's exactly what she wants."

Bruce agreed.

"Grrr," Heidi growled as they walked into the cafeteria and sat at their favorite table by the window.

"May I sit with you?" Heidi heard someone in front of her say.

She looked up from her lunch to see Bryce.

"Sure!" Heidi said and pointed to an empty chair across from hers. Then she quickly introduced Bryce to Lucy and Bruce. She didn't feel like talking after her run-in with Smell-a-nie, but luckily Lucy and Bruce did.

"So, how do you like Brewster so far?" Lucy asked.

Bryce pulled a strawberry yogurt from her lunch box and peeled back the lid. "The best part so far is being next-door neighbors with Heidi," she said.

Heidi smiled weakly and took a bite of her turkey sandwich.

"And how do you like your new teacher?" Bruce asked.

Bryce smiled. "She's fine."

Heidi dipped a carrot in ranch dressing, but before she could take a bite, the dressing dribbled onto her shirt.

"Ugh!" Heidi complained. "I need a napkin." She hopped up from the table to get one.

With Heidi gone, Bryce turned to Lucy and Bruce. "Hey, why didn't you offer Heidi one of *your* napkins? I thought you were Heidi's best friends."

Lucy and Bruce looked at each other helplessly.

"Oopsie," Lucy said. "Maybe we should have."

Bryce shrugged and asked, "So what's up with Heidi, anyway? She seems mad about something."

Lucy peeled her banana. "Well, she is a little mad," she said. "This girl in our class was mean to her on the way to lunch."

Bryce took a bite of her yogurt. "And did you stick up for Heidi? Best friends should ALWAYS stick up for each other."

Lucy swallowed uncomfortably.

Then Heidi sat down and dabbed at her shirt with a napkin. "Now it's smearing!" she complained.

Bryce pulled a wet wipe from her lunch box and offered it to Heidi. "Try this," she said.

Heidi took the wipe. "Thanks," she said, rubbing the spot on her top.

The stain disappeared. "It worked!" Heidi exclaimed. She balled up the wipe and tossed it in the garbage behind her. Then she shut her lunch box. "I'm done," she said.

Bryce closed her lunch box. "Me too! Do you want to go outside?"

"Yes, I do," Heidi said. Then she announced, "My new friend and I are going outside!"

The girls stood up and left.

Lucy and Bruce sat and watched them walking away.

"Ouch," Lucy said.

"Total ouch," added Bruce.

Heidi breathed in a great big breath of fresh air. "AHHH, it feels good to be outside."

Bryce linked her arm in Heidi's. "It sure does! Do you want to be my tour guide again and show me around the playground?"

Heidi stood up straight. "Just follow ME!"

The two friends galloped down the stairs and onto the blacktop. Heidi showed off the hopscotch first. They hopped across one. After that Heidi showed Bryce the ball wall, the foursquare court, the map of the United States, the monkey bars, and the basketball courts. Then they skipped to the swing sets.

"Swings are my favorite thing on the playground," Heidi said, plunking herself onto a blue rubber seat.

Bryce grabbed the chains and plopped onto a green one. "ME TOO!" she agreed.

The girls pumped their legs and squealed as they went higher and higher.

"You know what's crazy?" Heidi said. "Bruce doesn't even like to swing anymore!"

Bryce's mouth dropped open. "That's so WACKY!" she said. "I could

NEVER be friends with someone who didn't like to SWING."

Heidi laughed, but she knew she would always be friends with Bruce—even if he didn't like to swing. Then she pumped her legs two more times, jumped off the swing, and landed without falling.

Bryce scuffed the dirt with her boots to slow down the swing. "Way to go!" cheered. "I wish I could I'm too clumsy to la

Bryce took a smaller jump and almost landed it.

"It just takes practice—that's all," Heidi said.

Bryce nodded and pointed to a ball on the grass behind them.

"Look!" she cried. "Somebody left a soccer ball on the field. Let's play!"

She ran to the ball and kicked it to Heidi. It whizzed right by her.

"Ugh, sorry," Heidi said as she chased after the ball. "I STINK at soccer, but Lucy is a total star. One time in a practice game she faked me out so bad, I had grass stains on my skin!"

Heidi kicked the ball back, and Bryce stopped it with the sole of her boot.

"What kind of a friend does that?" Bryce questioned. "True friends would never ever embarrass each other like that on purpose."

Heidi tilted her head to one side. She didn't know what to say. It wasn't like Lucy had been trying to be mean to her. Or had she been?

The bell rang, and the girls ran back inside.

Heidi felt all mixed up.

What's the difference between a true friend and a best friend? she wondered.

Chapter 6

FRiEND OR FOE?

After school, Heidi spied Lucy, Bruce, and Bryce talking at the bus stop. *Oh yay!* she thought. *Now we can ALL be friends!* As she hurried along, Heidi noticed something weird. Lucy and Bruce were walking away from Bryce—and they both looked upset.

"What just happened?" Heidi asked Bryce when she reached the bus.

Bryce shrugged. "Beats me. I don't think Lucy and Bruce like me. They told me to stay away from you because you're THEIR best friend."

Heidi shook her head in disbelief.

"Uh, whoa, that does not sound like my friends at all."

Bryce nodded. "And that's what I told them. I said they didn't sound like they're your friends at all. After that, they stormed off. Lucy's mom is giving Bruce a ride home."

Heidi ran her hand through her hair, trying to understand what was going on.

"And do you know what they said
when I asked if we could have a ride
too?" Bryce went on.

Heidi shook her head slowly.

"They said, 'NO WAY.'"

Heidi's jaw dropped. She could not
believe what Bryce was saying.

Then the bus driver had to clap her hands sharply to make the girls look up.

"Are you two going to join us today?" the driver asked. "I'm closing the doors."

Heidi followed Bryce onto the bus.

Heidi still had no words, but Bryce sure did! She talked the entire way home.

"You want to come over?" Bryce asked when they got off the bus.

Heidi was *pooped*. "Sorry, I can't," she said. "I promised my mom I'd clean my room."

Bryce laughed as she walked back to her house. "Ha! Whatever you say, Cinderella!"

Heidi shuffled in through the back door and dumped her backpack on the floor.

Her mom came in and held out the phone.

"It's for you," she whispered.

Heidi put the phone to her ear. "Hello?"

"HELLO!" responded a loud voice.
It was Lucy. "We're both really MAD!"

"That's right!" added Bruce.

Then Lucy and Bruce both began
talking at the same time.

"WAIT!" interrupted
Heidi. "Will you guys
PUH-LEASE talk one at
a time?"

The phone went quiet for a moment. Then Lucy said, "Your new friend Bryce is NO GOOD. Do you know what she said to us at the bus stop?"

"Um, no," Heidi answered.

"She said YOU are HER new best friend," Lucy said. "And that you only PRETEND to be nice to us."

Heidi slumped into a kitchen chair.

"Bryce is SO mean," added Bruce. "If you're friends with her, then . . . then we can't be friends with you."

His words made Heidi stare at the phone in shock.

"You're going to have to CHOOSE, Heidi!" Lucy said. "It's either HER or US."

Chapter 7

COMPLiCATED

Heidi skipped her after-school snack and trudged upstairs to tidy her room.

Mom popped in her head a minute later. "Everything okay?"

Heidi crumpled an old math sheet and tossed it in the wastebasket.

"No. Not really," Heidi mumbled.

She plopped down on her bed. "Lucy and Bruce are mad at me." Then she told her mom about her weird day.

Mom sat down beside her. "True friends always come around," she said.

Heidi flopped onto her stomach. "What about BEST FRIENDS? I already have two best friends, and three is just too COMPLICATED."

Mom laughed and smiled. "It is complicated. But you have a great big heart, and I know there's room in there for all kinds of friends."

Then she ruffled Heidi's hair.

Heidi moaned.

"What you need is time to think about things," Mom said, heading for the door. "I know! Maybe the perfect solution will reveal itself as you clean up your room."

Heidi rolled off the bed and began to pick up her dirty clothes. That's when she noticed her *Book of Spells*.

She felt a twinge of hope. *Maybe there's a spell in there that will give me a vacation from friends to figure things out,* she thought.

Heidi opened the magic book and thumbed through the pages. She found a spell called All by Myself and read it over.

All by Myself

Are you finding it impossible to get along with your friends lately? Maybe it feels like everybody's mad at you. Do you secretly wish your friends would stop bugging you? If you'd like to get away from your people problems for a while, then this is the spell for you!

Ingredients:

1 picture of yourself alone

1 cornflake

1 sock

1 drawing of yourself

Mix the ingredients together in a bowl. Then hold your Witches of Westwick medallion in one hand and hold your other hand over the bowl. Chant the following spell:

To all my friends everywhere,

I need some peace and quiet.

Hide me from the world outside.

I'm on a social diet.

Heidi gathered the first three ingredients and sat down at her desk to draw a picture of herself. When she was done, she tossed everything into a bowl. Then she held her Witches of Westwick medallion in one hand, placed her other hand over the mix, and chanted the spell.

Heidi felt a warm glow wash over her. She yawned. Then she got ready for bed and fell fast asleep.

A FUNNY FEELING

Heidi sat up and looked at the clock.

Oh my gosh! she said to herself. *I'm going to be late for school!* She slid out of bed, got dressed, and ran downstairs to have breakfast. *That's weird,* she thought. *There are only three place mats on the table, and everyone has already eaten.* She opened the cupboard to grab the cereal. Then she remembered it was upstairs in her room. She decided to have yogurt.

Heidi stopped in front of the refrigerator door. *What? My picture is missing!* She felt the hair on the back of her neck stand up. But then she laughed. *Of course my picture is missing,* she said to herself. *It's SUPPOSED to be missing. I used it to cast my spell last night. Sheesh.*

"Five minutes till the bus comes!"
Mom called from her office.

Henry slammed the door to his
room. "Okay!" he called.

Heidi heard him clump down the
stairs and into the kitchen. He marched
right past her and didn't even say a
word. It was as if she wasn't there.

Huh, Heidi thought. Then she grabbed a granola bar, picked up her backpack, and followed her brother out the door.

The bus arrived on time, and Henry bounded up the steps. Heidi followed, and the doors folded shut on her. *Shmoosh!* Then they automatically reopened. Heidi blushed and checked

to see if anyone was laughing at her. Nobody seemed to notice.

She walked down the aisle and saw Bryce. But Bryce didn't even look up. She was talking to a girl from the other class. Heidi sat down in a seat all by herself. *Oh yay! I get to ride to school in peace today,* she thought. *No friends to smother me.*

As she looked out the window Heidi had a funny feeling. *I wonder if I'm invisible.*

Chapter 9

THE WHOLE THING

Lucy breezed past Heidi on the way to class. Then Bruce ran by her too. Neither of them said hi.

They're probably still mad, Heidi thought. She turned to go to class and crashed smack into Melanie. Melanie flopped flat on her rear in the middle

of the hallway. The kids in the hall
all laughed. Melanie's face turned
red as she stood up and stormed off.
She didn't say one thing to Heidi—or
even seem to notice that Heidi had
accidentally knocked her down.

Whoa, Heidi thought. *I really AM invisible. There's no way Melanie would pass up a chance to yell at me.*

As the bell rang, Heidi slipped into her classroom and sat down. She listened for her name during morning attendance, but Mrs. Welli skipped right over it.

Oh brother, Heidi thought. *This is going to be a LONG morning.*

"Okay, class, please pull out your historical heroes handout," Mrs. Welli said. "Now, let's see how well we know our heroes." She opened her book. "What did Rosa Parks refuse to do on the bus in Montgomery, Alabama?"

Heidi's hand shot
up, but Mrs. Welli
called on Melanie.

"Mrs. Rosa Parks
refused to give up
her seat to a white
person on the bus,"
Melanie said.

Mrs. Welli nodded. "And why was
that a bold move?" she asked.

Heidi raised her hand again, but
Mrs. Welli called on Stanley.

"Because African Americans had
been forced to sit at the back of the
bus," he said.

The teacher nodded and pointed to Eve Etsy. "Why did this make Rosa Parks a hero?" Mrs. Welli asked.

"Because she helped end *segre* . . . *segregation* on, umm, public transportation," said Eve.

The answers made Mrs. Welli clap her hands in approval. "That's right!"

Then the class talked about Abraham Lincoln, Martin Luther King, Jr., and Maya Angelou. Mrs. Welli didn't call on Heidi once.

At lunch, Heidi went straight to the playground and sat by herself. Soon the other kids began to come out. Melanie, Bryce, and Stanley ran to the swings. Heidi sipped her chocolate milk and watched.

"Here I go!" Bryce shouted. Then she leaped off the swing and landed on her feet—just like Heidi had done the day before.

Melanie and Stanley cheered for Bryce.

"It's the first time I've landed it!" Bryce said.

Heidi stuck her empty chocolate milk carton in her lunch box. *Good for Bryce,* she thought.

Then Melanie and Stanley jumped from their swings.

Heidi watched the three friends as they played together. *I feel so ALONE,* she thought. *Now I wish I hadn't cast that spell.* She sank lower on the bench and didn't even notice when Lucy and Bruce walked up. Her two friends sat down on the bench beside her.

"Is there something the matter, Heidi?" Lucy asked.

Heidi straightened up. "Wait, can you guys actually SEE me?"

Bruce laughed out loud. "Of course we can see you, silly. You're our best friend! Best friends always see each other."

Lucy scooted closer to Heidi. "We're really sorry about yesterday.

That was not a nice thing, to ask you to choose between friends."

Heidi sat up. "Can we just forget about the whole thing?"

Bruce looked both ways. "Forget about what thing?"

The girls both laughed.

"The WHOLE thing!" said Heidi.

And they did.

Chapter 10

F.R.I.E.N.D.S.

The next morning Heidi counted four place mats and four napkins at the table.

"Oh yay!" Heidi cried. "I STILL EXIST!"

Mom and Dad looked at each other.

"Of course you exist," Dad said.

"We were never in doubt."

Henry bounced a Super Ball on the floor and caught it. "Well, I exist too!" he said.

Heidi set the plates on the table. "That's not what I heard. I heard little brothers are going extinct, like the dinosaurs."

Henry put up his arms like a T. rex and stomped toward Heidi. "Not this one!"

Heidi hid behind a chair. Then she pounced on Henry when he got close. Everyone laughed.

On the bus Heidi sat next to Bryce.
"Hey, can I ask you something?" Heidi
said.

Bryce let her book bag slide to the
floor before she said, "Of course."

Heidi looked into Bryce's soft brown eyes. "I think you're really nice," she began, "so I just can't understand why you weren't very nice to Lucy and Bruce."

Bryce lowered her eyes for a moment. "Oh, I'm sorry, Heidi.

It's just so hard to come to a new school where everyone already has friends. I really wanted you to like me—that's all."

Heidi smiled. "I definitely like you! I'm sure you'll like Lucy and Bruce once you get to know them too."

Bryce smiled, but she didn't say anything about Lucy and Bruce. Instead, Bryce told Heidi about how she had landed the trick on the swing.

When they got to school, Heidi joined Lucy and Bruce on the playground. Bryce headed off with Melanie and Stanley. Heidi waved good-bye to Bryce.

Lucy noticed. "Hey, it looks like Bryce is making more friends," Lucy said.

"She is," Heidi said. "Oh, I talked to her about everything on the bus, and she feels bad about the way she acted."

"Well, that's good to hear," Lucy said.

Bruce agreed. "Yeah, but you know what's really been bugging me about Bryce?"

The girls shook their heads.

"Her name is only ONE letter off from MY name!" said Bruce. "Promise me you won't ever call me Bryce by mistake!"

Lucy and Heidi burst out laughing.

"We promise," said Heidi. "Let's hope we don't call Bryce BRUCE, either!"

Then all three friends let out the biggest *best friend* laughter.

And it felt *so* good.

Heidi and Lucy floppity-flopped onto Heidi's bed. The two best friends were playing a game of Would You? Could You?

"Your turn!" Heidi said.

Lucy propped herself up on one elbow. "Okay, I've got one," she said. "Would you? Could you? Umm, eat a chocolate-covered BUG?"

An excerpt from Heidi Heckelbeck and the Snoopy Spy

Heidi giggled and wrinkled her nose. *"Maybe,"* she said. "If the bug wasn't too crunchy. It is chocolate, after all."

Lucy squeezed her eyes shut. "GROSS!" she cried.

Both girls cracked up.

"Okay, my turn," Heidi said. "Would you? Could you? Dump a whole bottle of strawberry shampoo on Melanie Maplethorpe's head?"

Both girls squealed.

"That's funny," Lucy said, catching her breath. "But a teeny bit mean."

Heidi shoved Lucy playfully. "It's

not MEAN, it's CLEAN!" she said. "Get it? *Shampoo?*"

The two girls started laughing again.

"Okay, here's a good one," Lucy said. "Would you? Could you? Ask Stanley Stonewrecker to go to a movie?"

Heidi's cheeks turned red. Then she leaned in closer to Lucy.

She whispered loudly, "Yes!"

Lucy shrieked, and both girls collapsed in laughter again.

"I knew it!" Lucy cried. "I knew it all the time!"

An excerpt from *Heidi Heckelbeck and the Snoopy Spy*